ISHKADOODLE

A Boy, His Vacuum &
Their Outerspace Adventure

WRITTEN BY JONATHAN J. ARKING

ILLUSTRATED & DESIGNED BY JOSHUA WERNER

ISBN 978-0-692-18150-8

This book is dedicated to my three children; Joshua, Emily and Claire, whose giggles at bedtime and cries of "Tell one more Daddy" will always be some of my most cherished memories.

— Jon

To Josie and Cody — may your friendship always be as strong and adventurous as the one found within this book.

— Josh

Ishkadoodle loved vacuum cleaners. He was fascinated by them. He loved the sound they made, like a racecar, and the way they looked like a rocket ship on the launch pad, ready to blast into orbit! But most of all, he loved the way they could clean up almost any mess he made.

Ishkadoodle had a favorite vacuum. He called it Vroomy. It was tall, blue, and had an extra-long hose. Wherever Ishkadoodle went, Vroomy went with him. If he went to the park, Vroomy helped to clean up litter. If he went to the store, Vroomy helped to carry out the bags. And when he went to school, Vroomy always kept his desk neat.

One sunny day, Ishkadoodle and Vroomy headed to the park. When they arrived, Ishkadoodle noticed a large crowd had gathered around a man. He wondered what it was all about.

The man was asking the crowd for volunteers to go on a special trip. "Who wants to go into outer space? We have monthly missions and need people for these once-in-a-lifetime opportunities!" his voice echoed through the speaker.

Almost everyone raised their hands, some jumping up and down, while others yelled, "Pick me! Pick me!" Ishkadoodle also wanted to go, but when he raised his hand, no one could see him. Not wanting to be left out, he climbed to the top of Vroomy and again raised his hand. Now he was taller than everyone else!

"I see an eager hand!" said the man. "Let me see this brave person."

Ishkadoodle stepped forward.

The man began to frown. "Why, you're just a boy. I applaud your bravery young man, but we need grown-ups to go into space." He patted Ishkadoodle on the head and nudged him back into the crowd.

Ishkadoodle was mad. He wanted to go into space. So what if he was a kid? Kids were brave too!

As he sat with Vroomy, Ishkadoodle noticed the man's truck parked nearby. That gave him an idea! If he couldn't go into space, he could at least see the rocket. And that truck was sure to take him there.

With Vroomy at his side, Ishkadoodle snuck over to the truck. Inside, he found a large box and carefully climbed in. He pulled the lid shut and sat in silence, waiting for what seemed like forever. Finally, he heard the roar of the engine. The truck was moving and he and Vroomy were bouncing around in the box.

"Maybe this wasn't such a good idea after all," Ishkadoodle thought.

When the truck stopped, he considered hopping out, but before he could, he felt the box being lifted. Where were they *going?*

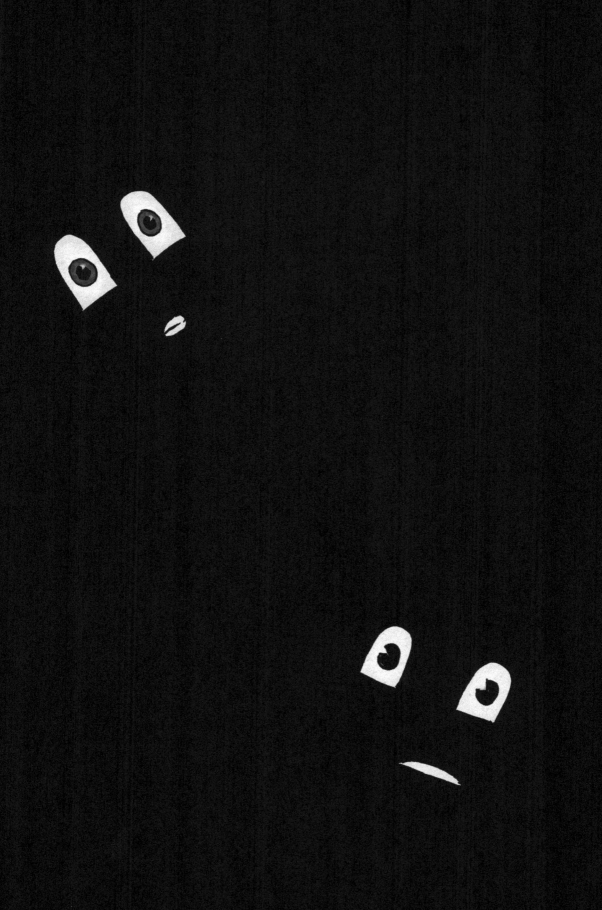

After a few minutes, the box was set down. Then it was very quiet. Until . . . he thought he heard a faint noise. He listened very hard. And then: **"10, 9, 8, 7 . . ."** Someone was reading off numbers through a speaker. **"6, 5, 4 . . ."** It was a countdown!

Ishkadoodle was excited. This must be the rocket launch! He wanted to see, so he lifted the lid just enough to peek and saw that he was . . .

INSIDE THE SPACESHIP!

The box began to shake and rumble until the lid fell off. Now Ishkadoodle could see that two astronauts were busy at the controls. They didn't even notice him. Up, up, up went the spaceship. Soon the bright, blue sky gave way to the deep dark of outer space. Ishkadoodle began to feel funny. Something was different. He was floating! Then he remembered reading that in outer space, people become weightless as gravity disappears. Gravity is the force that keeps people and things on the ground back on Earth.

Just then, one of the astronauts turned around and saw Ishkadoodle. He couldn't believe his eyes. "Who are you?" he asked angrily.

Ishkadoodle didn't know what to say. He was excited to be on the spaceship, but he knew he was in big trouble. A loud alarm bell suddenly started to ring. **KLANG, KLANG, KLANG.**

The other astronaut turned and yelled, "We've got a problem with the booster engine! There's not enough thrust!"

The first astronaut looked at the control panel and then looked right at Ishkadoodle. "That's because there's extra weight on board we hadn't counted on." Uh oh.

Inspecting the panel, the other astronaut said, "The fuel pump is plugged up! What do we do?" Mission Control called over the radio, "You've got to find some way to suck it out or you're going to crash!"

"Wow," thought Ishkadoodle, "this IS serious."

But then he had an idea.

He reached behind and pulled out Vroomy. The astronauts looked at each other and then back at Ishkadoodle. A vacuum cleaner! Of course! That's just what they needed!

Taking Vroomy's hose, Ishkadoodle rushed over to the fuel pump and began cleaning it out. The alarm stopped ringing. The astronauts cheered, "Hooray for Ishkadoodle and Vroomy!"

Even though the problem was fixed, the astronauts didn't want to take any chances. Soon they had turned the spaceship around and were heading back to Earth.

As the clouds came into view, Ishkadoodle's excitement faded. He wasn't supposed to be on this rocket. Was he going to be grounded? He didn't feel much like a hero.

When the rocket landed, Ishkadoodle noticed a crowd had gathered near the launch pad. They were cheering Ishkadoodle!

As he walked down the ramp with Vroomy, the crowd rushed over to congratulate him. They were smiling and shouting.

Ishkadoodle was happy too, but he needed to get home — he didn't want to be late for dinner! Finally, he managed to slip away.

Ishkadoodle couldn't keep the smile off of his face. What a day! There's no telling what a boy and his vacuum cleaner can do!

THE END.

About the Author: Jon Arking is a radio broadcaster, podcaster and all-around swell guy. He and his wife Carolyn live in Howell, Michigan with their three children.

About the Artist: Josh Werner lives with his family in America's Mitten, where he spends endless hours diving into one creative project after another, in his diabolical attempt to infect the world with his special brand of eccentricity.

CPSIA information can be obtained
at www.ICGtesting.com
Printed in the USA
BVHW021029181121
621925BV00011B/572

9 780692 181508